Published by Puffin 2014
A Penguin Company
Penguin Books Ltd, 80 Strand, London, WC2R 0RL, UK
Penguin Group (USA) Inc., 375 Hudson Street, New York 10014, USA
Penguin Books Australia Ltd, 707 Collins Street, Melbourne, Victoria 3008,
Australia (A division of Pearson Australia Group Pty Ltd)
Canada, India, New Zealand, South Africa

Written by Richard Dungworth
Illustrated by Richard Jones – Beehive Illustration Agency

www.puffinbooks.com

ISBN: 978-0-14135-435-4
001
Printed and bound in Great Britain by Clays Ltd, St Ives plc

DOCTOR FOSSIL

CHARLIE PEPPER

PUFFIN

Contents

Prologue

Somewhere in a distant dimension, beneath a sky the colour of an ugly bruise, a tiny island of rock floated in a sea of poisonous cloud. At the centre of this barren Sky Prison stood its captive – the caped figure of Lord Tenoroc, overlord of all Super Villains, and terror of the Multiverse.

Despite his grim surroundings, Tenoroc wore a wicked smile. His yellow eyes were fixed on a small, hexagonal disc hovering in the air in front of him.

'Ah . . . *yes* . . .'

Tenoroc studied the disc as it slowly twirled and flipped. Its gold edges framed the image of a man – or, at least, a man-like being. Instead of hair, his

head was covered in feathery silver plumes.
He had knobbly ridged skin like that of a reptile.
A large amber jewel was set deep in the centre
of his scrawny chest.

'*Doctor Fossil*!' hissed Tenoroc. 'He with the
awesome power to resurrect prehistoric monsters . . .'

Tenoroc had taken his time selecting this particular Life Cell. He was determined to choose well. His collection of stolen Cells offered his only chance of escaping the Sky Prison. Each one contained the captured holographic form of a fearsome Super Villain. These black-hearted, super-powered scoundrels all recognized Tenoroc as their master. He had only to set them loose, back into the Multiverse, to employ their sinister talents.

And soon, I shall release them all! thought Tenoroc. Then the Multiverse will crumble − and I will break free of this cursed dimension!

For now, however, his powers were weakened. It would take all his strength to release the occupant of a single Cell.

But Fossil will be enough! gloated Tenoroc. He alone will create chaos, at my command!

With a wave of one bony hand, he began the process of setting loose his servant. The Life Cell drifted across to hover over a device that stood on a table of rock close by. This was Tenoroc's Triple Sphere, the instrument through which

he channelled his mystical powers – three stacked orbs of Star Crystal, topped and tailed with lethal spikes.

'Time to bring to life . . .' snarled Tenoroc, '*A BRINGER OF LIFE*!'

He raised his hand once more, preparing to begin the final phase of the Super Villain's reactivation . . .

. . . when the drama of the moment was shattered by a fit of high-pitched giggling right behind him.

'Tee-hee-hee, oh-ho-ho, ha-ha-ha!'

Tenoroc turned, scowling.

A gargoyle – an ugly winged beast carved from stone – perched nearby. Unlike most stone carvings, this one was unquestionably alive. The strangely cute little creature was holding its sides and waggling its stunted wings as it shook with laughter.

'Oh . . . hee-hee . . . *bring to life* . . . ho-ho . . . *a bringer of life* . . . tee-hee . . . I . . . I see what you did there!' it squealed. 'You *kill* me, my Lord!'

Tenoroc's scowl deepened. '*That* can be

arranged, Craw,' he snarled.

For once, his grovelling underling caught on quickly. Craw stopped laughing, gulped and hurriedly put on his best stony-serious face.

Tenoroc turned back to the Triple Sphere. With another gesture, he sent the floating Life Cell drifting down into a socket in the device's upper surface. The Cell flared with light.

'Doctor Fossil . . .' hissed Tenoroc, eyes blazing. He gave a dramatic sweep of his arm, fingers curled like claws. Life-force poured from the glowing Cell, forming swirls of luminous green in the upper orb of the Sphere. It trickled through to the larger central orb, which began to crackle and spit with intense white light.

'. . . *ARISE*!' bellowed Tenoroc.

Relic Gorge was as silent as the grave.

A grave, in fact, was exactly what the gorge was. The remote canyon, deep in the hot desert

wilderness of the Sea of Sands, was the resting place of countless prehistoric beasts. They had died many millions of years ago. Their bones had been preserved in the gorge's layered rock, as fossils.

And fossils had brought fossil-hunters. The gorge's present day landscape had all the features of a major scientific dig – wooden scaffolds, ramps and ladders, shovels and buckets and several neat, orderly excavations.

What it *didn't* have right now was any sign of activity. There wasn't a soul around.

But that was about to change.

Sticking out from the rock face of one of the gorge's walls was the strangest of all its fossils. It was the fossilized body of a man. A pinprick of fiery light suddenly pierced its stony surface. The light-spot quickly spread. Within seconds, the whole body was ablaze. With a final flare of light, it came alive.

The reanimated man tumbled to the ground. Slowly, he got to his feet. He looked around, muttering.

'What . . . in the name . . . of Natural Selection . . . ?'

He was an odd-looking individual, with a skeletal face, pitted skin and silvery, feather-like hair. His right hand was covered by a strange electro-mechanical glove. Thick yellow cables ran from its fingertips into the sleeve of his military shirt. He wore camo-combat trousers, kneepads and boots. His deep-set eyes were blood red.

As he took in his surroundings, his face lit up.

'I . . . I'm *back*!' he gasped. 'It's my dig! Just as I left it!'

He jumped down into the nearest and largest of the excavated pits, and dropped to his knees in front of the fossilized dinosaur skeleton that lay uncovered within it.

'My beautiful specimens!' he cried. 'They're still here! My work continues!'

A moment later, his look of delight turned to one of terror, as a thunderous voice echoed around the gorge.

'*FOSSIL!*'

An unnatural bank of dark cloud hung directly above the gorge, in an otherwise clear blue sky. The form of a nightmarish face was visible within it. Doctor Fossil looked up to meet its angry stare.

'Lord Tenoroc!'

'I did not free you to pursue your scientific dreams!' snarled Tenoroc's scowling cloud-image.

'How may I serve you, lord?'

'Find and reanimate the ultimate demon beast!' roared Tenoroc. '*So I can spread chaos in the Multiverse!*'

As the echoes of his voice died away, Tenoroc's image, and the clouds from which it had been formed, dissolved to nothingness.

Doctor Fossil looked thoughtful. 'The ultimate beast . . .' he muttered to himself, getting to his feet. 'Hmmm. That might take some time to find.'

His red eyes settled once more on the fossilized skeleton that lay before him. A wicked grin spread across his face.

'But *you*, Eoraptor, can start the chaos!'

Cackling madly, Fossil threw back his arms and raised his face to the blue sky. A fiery amber

glow flared beneath his shirt. Streams of crackling energy suddenly burst from his chest. They leapt at the dinosaur bones, like arcs of lightning.

As Fossil's wild laughter echoed around Relic Gorge, it was joined by a chorus of inhuman screeches, coming from within the pit . . .

1
Math(s) Problems

Matt blew the dust from the top of the cardboard box, and set about untying its bindings. The string was so old it snapped as he tugged at the first knot. He folded back the box's flaps and peered inside.

'Hey, Marlon! Check this out!'

In answer to Matt's call, a tiny furry head popped up from a pile of dismantled gaslights in the corner of the storeroom. Marlon, Matt's pet dwarf Tasmanian devil, came scampering across to see what new treasure his best friend had found.

It was several months now since Matt and his parents, Harry and Meg Hatter, had moved from

New York to London, to help his grandfather run the famous Notting Hill Coronet movie theatre. Even so, Matt's explorations of his new home continued to turn up exciting surprises on a daily basis. The theatre's ground floor storeroom was his favourite hunting ground. The Hatters who had run the Coronet over the last century – Matt's Grandpa Alfred and late Great-grandpa Samuel – had used the little room to stash away every bit of out-dated equipment or movie memorabilia from their time in charge. For a movie-mad teen like Matt the junk-crammed space was a paradise.

Marlon chittered excitedly as he watched Matt remove a dozen round metal film canisters, one at a time, from inside the box.

'*Pandora* . . . *Cyber Racer* . . . *Werewolf King* . . .' Matt's eyes sparkled as he read each faded label in turn. 'These are classics, Marlon, from *way* back! Even I haven't seen most of the movies in here! How cool would it be if we could get Dad to show them on Screen One, just for us?'

Marlon's squeal implied it would be *very* cool.

'Or *maybe* . . .' Matt looked across to where an antique film projector lay among the clutter. '. . . maybe if I twist his arm, he might get that old thing running again.' Harry Hatter loved tinkering with anything mechanical. 'We could project these onto our bedroom wall!'

Marlon chittered his approval.

'We just need to see if we can catch Dad when he's in a really good mood . . .'

'*MATTHEW LUKE HATTER*!'

The holler of a voice along the corridor outside made Matt wince.

'Which isn't now, by the sounds of it,' he told Marlon. 'Dad using my full name always spells trouble.' He quickly replaced the film canisters, then made his way towards the doorway. 'You keep looking around, little buddy. I'll go see what I've done wrong *this* time . . .'

Matt had left his skateboard leaning up outside the storeroom door. With a practised flick of his foot, he flipped it up-and-over on to its wheels. He stepped on and kicked off.

'Coming, Dad!'

One of the many things Matt loved about the Coronet was the theatre's long stretches of smoothly carpeted floor – perfect for indoor skating. There were some neat spots for jumps, too. The three-step drop into the lobby, up ahead, was one of Matt's favourites.

Let's give it plenty of air, thought Matt to himself, building speed. It was only as he kicked off from the top step that he noticed the giant figure in the centre of the lobby. It was a cardboard cutout of the half-human, half-robot hero of the latest sci-fi blockbuster, *Robo-Enforcer*. It was standing right where Matt had intended to land.

'*Whooooaaaahh!*'

Matt, on his airborne skateboard, sailed straight into the cardboard cyborg. The resulting wipe-out was even more spectacular than his jump. Cardboard body parts flew in all directions.

Matt slowly picked himself up – to find that he was now wearing Robo-Enforcer's top half around his neck. His head had burst right through the cyborg's armoured chest.

'Matt! Are you *crazy*?'

His mum was standing by the ticket counter, looking at his handiwork in disbelief. His dad was beside her. Matt's heart sank. A double-parent-talking-to was never good news. It wasn't going to help that he had just trashed the lobby display.

'But . . . Dad used my middle name!' he protested. 'He only does that when I'm in big trouble. So . . . so I thought I should come *quickly*.'

His dad shook his head. 'You aren't in "big trouble"!' he said cheerily. Then his smile faltered. 'Or at least you *weren't* – until you destroyed Robo-Enforcer . . .'

'Matthew.' Matt's mum held up a typewritten document, the sight of which made his spirits sink even further. 'We're concerned about your grades.'

'Ah. My report card.' Matt looked shifty. 'Didn't realize it had arrived.' Judging by his mum's 'concerned' look, Matt guessed his school report was every bit as bad as he'd feared. Or worse. He began to retreat, moving robot-style, towards the lobby steps.

'*Good-bye, ci-ti-zens*!' droned Matt, swinging his cyborg arms. '*I have an e-mer-gen-cy to a-ttend to.*'

His mum was having none of it.

'Power down, Robo-Enforcer!' she said with a wry smile.

Matt ground to a robotic halt, as if someone had pulled his plug.

'Matt,' said his dad patiently, 'we're most concerned about maths.'

Matt pulled a face. 'Math-*sss*?' he echoed. He had been having enough trouble getting to grips with how his new English classmates talked – like being invited to play "football at break",

instead of soccer at recess. He could do without
his dad falling back into his old English ways.
'Back in New York, there was no "s" in "math"!'
Matt looked to his mum – a born-and-bred New
Yorker – for support.

'As far as we're concerned,' smiled his dad,
pointing at the report card, 'there's no "D" in it
either, Mister!'

'Which is why . . .' his mum followed up
'. . . Mrs Crumpepper is on her way over – to
tutor you.'

Matt's mood hit rock bottom. His hopes of
spending the evening happily rooting around the
storeroom with Marlon evaporated.

'Not The *Crumpepper*!'

Mrs Crumpepper was an old friend of Matt's
grandfather. His dad had first suggested her as a
home tutor because he had occasionally been taught
by her himself, when he was a boy. *Which makes her
about a billion years old*, thought Matt.

'All I ever *do* is study!' he groaned. 'It's like
I'm . . .' He resumed his robot impersonation,

'. . . *Ro-bo-Stu-dent*!'

His dad gave him a look. 'Robo-Student would have got better grades!'

Matt may not have been top of the class lately, but he was smart enough to know when there was no point in arguing. He could usually talk his dad round, but even an ultra-tough law-enforcing cyborg would have been no match for his mum once she'd made up her mind. It looked like he had an appointment with The Crumpepper, whether he liked it or not.

Sulkily, Matt extracted himself from the remains of Robo-Enforcer, retrieved his skateboard and trudged off to tell Marlon the bad news.

2

Ambushed!

Captain Yasser of the Sultan's Guard had led camel caravans across the Sea of Sands many times before. For some reason, however, this particular desert trek was giving him the jitters.

The captain put his nervousness down to the value of his cargo. Between them, his team of six triple-humped camels were carrying more of the Sultan's worldly wealth than Yasser cared to think about.

But he couldn't help feeling there was something else – something about this particular region of the desert. For the last mile or so, he'd had the unsettling sense of being watched. And something

was definitely spooking the camels. Out of the
corner of an eye, Yasser caught a slight movement.

'Wha–?'

The lead camel had seen it, too. With a snort
of alarm, it reared up. 'Easy now, my precious,'
said Yasser, keeping tight hold of the beast's bridle.
He stroked the camel's side soothingly. 'Don't
worry. It's probably just a desert rat.'

Nevertheless, Yasser reached for his scimitar,
and drew the broad, curving blade from its sheath.

A strange chirruping animal call came from somewhere away to his right. Another answered from behind him.

'Huh?'

Yasser spun round, sword at the ready . . .

. . . but completely unprepared for the terrifying sight that met his eyes.

He barely had time to scream before the nightmarish beasts were upon him.

3
A Call for Help

Matt climbed the last few steps of the spiral staircase to his top-floor turret bedroom. He slumped on the end of his bed and let out a sigh. Marlon hopped up beside him. The little Tasmanian devil gazed up at his friend with concern.

'I can't *believe* they're sending over The Crumpepper to tutor me,' said Matt glumly.

Marlon chittered sympathetically.

It seemed totally unfair to Matt that his parents were hassling him about his report. It was true, of course, that his grades had slipped a little since he'd moved to London. It had taken time for him to find his feet at his new school, make new friends, get used to the English way of doing and saying things, and none of this had helped his schoolwork.

Plus I've got the Multiverse to take care of, thought Matt.

The countless surprises of the Coronet's storeroom were nothing compared to the one mind-blowing, life-changing discovery Matt had made on his very first day in his new home. The Coronet, he had been astonished to find, concealed a gateway to another dimension. This was the Multiverse – a place of wonder, danger and adventure.

Sadly, it was also a place where the Coronet was spoken of with dread. A century ago, in the days of Matt's great-grandfather, Samuel Hatter, the Coronet's Screen Two had shown classic adventure and monster movies daily. Samuel had never dreamt that by screening these movies, he was giving the Super Villains they featured a chance to escape, through the inter-dimensional portal, into the Multiverse. Here, the movie villains assumed physical form, becoming real beings. They had brought chaos to the Multiverse's twelve realms.

But the coming of the Hatter Heroes had turned the evil tide. Samuel Hatter had eventually discovered the catastrophic consequences of his Screen Two showings. Vowing to make amends, he had entered the Multiverse himself, and dedicated his life to capturing the marauding Super Villains, one by one. His son – Matt's Grandpa Alfred – had continued his work, until each and every Coronet Villain was safely imprisoned in a Life Cell.

A new, greater enemy, however, then arose, in the terrifying form of Lord Tenoroc. Tenoroc managed to steal the Life Cells. He planned to release their Super Villains to do his evil bidding – and destroy the Multiverse. In an epic one-on-one struggle, Alfred Hatter managed to thwart Tenoroc, locking him away in an isolated prison dimension – though doing so meant bravely accepting the same fate himself. With Alfred trapped, the Multiverse had been left without a champion . . .

. . . until Matt, in search of his grandfather, had blundered through the portal on his first day

at the Coronet. Now the role of Hatter Hero
had fallen to *him*.

Matt wondered if his parents might have been
more understanding if they'd known that as well as
homework, he had the fate of another world resting
on his thirteen-year-old shoulders.

Trouble is, I can't tell them . . .

Matt tried to put thoughts of the Multiverse
aside, so as to focus on his immediate problem.

'We need a plan to save us from The
Crumpepper,' he told Marlon. 'There has to be
some way out . . .' He fell silent, thinking hard.

Marlon, too, looked thoughtful. He stroked
his chin with a tiny paw, frowning.

Before either of them could come up with
an idea, their concentration was broken by the
outbreak of a high-pitched bleeping noise.

The alert sound was coming from a large,
leather-bound book that lay face-up on Matt's bed.
The Interactive Chronicles of Action and Adventure was
no ordinary book. It was Matt's discovery of the
Chronicles that had kicked off his amazing exploits

in the Multiverse. Its front cover had a hexagonal amber jewel set in its centre, which right now was glowing brightly. Matt hurriedly reached to press it. The bleeping stopped. With a flare of golden light, the jewel began to project a three-dimensional holographic image, which hovered just above it. It was a miniature likeness of a crimson-haired girl in a purple martial arts-style outfit.

'Roxie!'

The girl in the projection was one of two close friends Matt had made in the Multiverse. She was a feisty, fearless Tracker, his fellow adventurer – and occasional critic.

'Matt!' cried holo-Roxie. 'Big trouble in the Sea of Sands. Get down here – *now*!'

As abruptly as it had appeared, the projection vanished. The jewel's amber light faded to a gentle glimmer.

In a flash, Matt was his usual self, bursting with all-action energy. He snatched up the *Chronicles* and sprang from his bed, beaming.

'Saved by a different dimension!'

Roxie's call for help provided the perfect get-out. Matt wasn't about to turn his back on his Multiverse friends to keep an appointment with The Crumpepper. But *someone* would have to deal with her . . .

'Marlon . . .' Matt addressed his furry pal sincerely. 'Cover for me!'

Marlon was always ready to take on an assignment, however tough, to help his best friend. With a determined squeak, he gave Matt a tiny thumbs-up.

Satisfied that he was leaving the Crumpepper situation in good hands – or paws – Matt raced for the staircase. With the *Chronicles* tucked under one arm, he vaulted the bannister, and flew down the spiralling steps, heading at top speed for the doorway to a different dimension.

4
Hero Time

Matt took the last flight of stairs the fastest way he knew – by riding the spiralling bannister. As soon as his feet touched the first-floor landing, he was racing towards the large bookcase that occupied an alcove in its wall. He still had firm hold of the *Chronicles*. The book's cover jewel was now pulsing with golden light.

As Matt approached the bookcase, a second hexagon of amber, inset above its top shelf, answered the cover jewel by starting to flash and bleep. The entire bookcase suddenly began to rotate, like a revolving door. Matt quickly ducked through the revealed entrance. A moment later,

the bookcase completed its 360-degree spin, and the hidden doorway was sealed once more.

Matt now stood at one end of the corridor that led to the Coronet's secret second auditorium. Screen Two had been closed off many years ago. Since then, the Hatter Heroes alone had known of its continued existence. It gave Matt a buzz to think that only Great-grandpa Samuel and Grandpa Alfred had shared the secret of the revolving bookcase.

Matt held out the *Chronicles*, and thumped the amber hexagon inset in the centre of its cover. The jewel popped up from its brass-and-glass mounting, like the knob of a control dial. Matt grabbed it and twisted it clockwise one sixth of a turn.

'Time to dive into the Sea of Sands!'

Beneath the glowing jewel and its transparent surround, a mechanism of ghostly cogs and wheels began to whirr. The brass cover clasp clicked undone. The pages of the book swung open, releasing a blaze of amber light, and it rose free of Matt's hands. As it came to hover in front of his

face, something emerged from its dazzling pages –
a pair of ultra-cool shades, with one red lens and
one blue.

The Multivision Specs – the first essential piece
of Hatter Hero gear – drifted across to settle on
Matt's nose. He felt a familiar tingle as their DNA-
lock kicked in. The Specs had recognized their
owner – the only person for whom they would
work their magic.

The *Chronicles* suddenly shot away along the
corridor. As it went, it ejected the rest of Matt's
Multiverse equipment, in holographic form –
a cool action outfit; a neat pair of gloves; an
explorer's backpack. The holograms hung in the
wispy light-trail left behind by the *Chronicles*, which
had now disappeared through the doors at the
corridor's end.

Matt set off along the corridor at a sprint. As he
reached each hovering hologram, he leapt, lunged
or twisted to move through it – and instantly became
reclothed in the real thing. By the time he reached
the end of the corridor, he was fully kitted out.

Or *almost* fully. Last, but by no means least, came the Cell Blaster. Matt grabbed at its shimmering hologram and felt another tingling thrill as it took solid form in his grasp. Like the Multivision Specs, the Cell Blaster was locked to the unique DNA of the current Hatter Hero. In non-Hatter hands, it was useless. In Matt's, it was a multi-function weapon and super-gadget rolled into one.

Without slowing, Matt stowed the Blaster beneath his backpack. With his transformation from schoolboy to hero complete, he burst through the double doors into the Screen Two auditorium. The rows of red seating were eerily lit by the intense purple glare of the screen itself. A whirlpool of dazzling energy swirled at its centre. This was the Hatters' great secret – the inter-dimensional portal that led to the Multiverse. At its heart, the *Chronicles* blazed invitingly, lighting the way.

Matt sprinted down the aisle towards the front row, crouched to spring, then launched himself head first into the portal. He grasped the glowing book in both hands, and immediately felt it tug him

fiercely forward. As it dragged him into the depths of the swirling vortex, Matt clung on and prepared to enjoy the ride.

5
The Sea of Sands

The sand-surfer skimmed across the golden desert, cutting a path between the smooth rolling dunes that rose all around it like giant waves of sand, some with crests nearly ten metres high. The little craft was making good speed, despite there being only a gentle breeze to fill its single sail. Its secret was its lightweight build. Its narrow, boat-like body, from pointed prow at the front to squared-off stern at the back, was made from canvas stretched over timber struts. It ran on two large spoked rear wheels and a single front surfing skid. It was ideal for navigating the vast desert expanse of the Sea of Sands.

'Are we nearly there yet?'

A boy in a green hooded tunic and head-band was reclining in the back of the sand-surfer, enjoying the ride. For Allejandro Diego Gomez Monteros – plain 'Gomez' to his friends – such a relaxed attitude was far from typical. Gomez spent most of his time being frightened of things.

'I *think* so . . .' replied his female companion, who sat further forward in the surfer, doing all the hard work. She was using the craft's steering handle to control the position and angle of its sail. Piloting a sand-surfer was a tricky business, but Roxana Alexis, number one Tracker, was a natural. Roxie could read the wind like she could read a trail – instinctively, and better than anyone.

'Yup, I'm fairly sure we *must* be nearly there,' said Roxie. 'Only it's hard to be certain, when we don't know exactly where "there" is!'

'The directions were a bit hazy, weren't they?' admitted Gomez. 'But hey – you're a Tracker, Rox. You don't need directions!'

Back in Al-Harbar – the walled desert town

from which Roxie and Gomez had set out earlier that morning – they had asked several townsfolk about the whereabouts of Relic Gorge. All had known its name well, but not one had been able 1to pinpoint its precise location. Some of the Al-Harbarians had been reluctant to speak of the gorge at all. The desert region within which it lay

had something of a reputation. According to the locals, bad things happened there.

So when a terrified captain of the Sultan's Guard had come staggering through the gates of Al-Harbar the previous day, wailing that his camel caravan had been attacked – by *dinosaurs*, no less – the townsfolk had been unsurprised to hear that the doomed caravan had been somewhere in the region of Relic Gorge at the time.

'Any idea what's meant to be so bad about the place?' Roxie asked Gomez. 'I thought it was just famous for its fossils, right? How come everyone is so keen to steer clear?'

As a Keeper, Gomez was an expert on the various cultures of the Multiverse. He was only too happy to show off what he knew about Al-Habarian folklore.

'Relic Gorge has something of a dark past,' he told Roxie. 'It's said that long ago, before you and I were born, it served as the lair of a dangerous lunatic.' Gomez lowered his voice. '*A man who could summon ferocious monsters!*'

Roxie looked intrigued. '*Dino*-type monsters?'

Gomez shrugged. 'All I know is that Alfred Hatter got involved. He was just getting the hang of being Hatter Hero. They say he had a big showdown with some villain or other at the gorge. There's been no trouble since – but the locals still stay away.'

Roxie frowned. 'I'll bet old Mister Monster Maker was one of Tenoroc's cronies,' she said. 'But no long-gone loony is going to put *me* off. The gorge is where we need to start, I'm certain. Captain Yasser was pretty sure he and his camels were near it when they were attacked. And if he's right about *what* attacked . . . well, I can't think of a better place to look for dinosaurs than Relic Gorge, can you?'

The mention of Tenoroc had made Gomez sit up straight. He began to look more like his usual twitchy self.

'I guess not,' he said. 'But I hope Matt gets a move on. If there's any chance we're going to run into a bunch of prehistoric predators, I'd feel a lot happier with a Hatter Hero at my side!'

'In front of you, more like!' laughed Roxie. 'And don't worry – Matt got my call. He'll be here.'

Gomez smiled to himself. It wasn't that long since he had first shown Roxie how to use her Tracker's staff to send a signal to Matt in his own dimension. Now she was proud to find it second nature. But Roxie had yet to discover even half of what her staff could do. Only Gomez, whose task it had been to provide the staff, knew the true range of its powers. It wasn't just the staff's amber jewel that pulsed with mystical energy. Its wooden shaft had been carved from the last branch of the Tree of Life, sacred among Keepers. Gomez had yet to reveal this to Roxie. He was waiting for the right time.

'*See?*' Roxie pointed into the distance. 'What did I tell you?'

Gomez looked – and saw a familiar purple swirl forming high in the sky, some way ahead. The portal was opening. As its mouth widened, it began to snake lower, like a tornado touching down.

'One Hatter Hero, heading our way!' cried

Roxie cheerfully. She expertly
adjusted the sand-surfer's
course, sending it racing
across the sand to intercept
the portal's swooping dive.

6
Mind the Boom!

Matt's Multiverse landings had improved a lot recently. His first, unexpected portal ride had not ended well. A messy crash-landing had left him flat on his face in the dust. He was proud to have managed nearly half a dozen (fairly) solid and (mostly) painless touchdowns since. He liked to think they'd been increasingly stylish, too.

Now, however, as Matt burst from the portal's mouth into clear blue sky, it seemed all too likely that his streak of safe landings was about to come to an end.

A sail-powered vehicle was racing across the golden desert that stretched below him. It was heading straight for the spot towards which he was falling fast. From his previous visits to the Sea of Sands, Matt recognized it as a sand-surfer. Knowing what it was didn't make him feel any happier about the fact that it was about to mow him down.

'*Aaaaaaaaaaaaaaaaaahhhh* . . .!'

Yelling and flailing his arms, Matt dropped helplessly into the vehicle's path . . .

. . . and landed, with a thump, on the sand-surfer's narrow prow. For a moment, he teetered there, almost managing to get his balance. He just had chance to see who was riding the speeding surfer before a dip-and-rise in its motion sent him toppling overboard.

As he fell, Matt clutched hopelessly at thin air. To his great surprise and relief he caught hold of Roxie's trusty wooden combat staff. Somehow, Roxie had managed to unsheathe and extend it in time to block his fall. She'd done all this with one hand, while controlling the surfer with the other. When it came to multi-tasking, Roxie was in a league of her own.

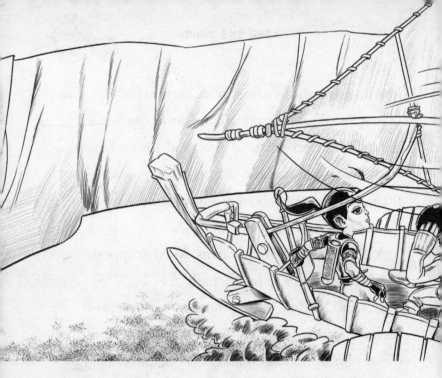

With the staff's help, Matt regained his balance
on the surfer. He clung to its sturdy boom as the
little craft continued to race across the sand.

'*Roxie!*' Matt gave his friend an exasperated
look, yelling to her over the sound of the air
rushing past. '*You call me down on to a moving
sand-surfer?*'

Roxie didn't appear to hear. She was staring
straight past Matt, and her violet eyes had grown
suddenly wide. She had just spotted a deep desert
crevasse only a little way ahead.

'Matt!' yelled Roxie, taking urgent action.
'Mind the boom!' She thrust the sand-surfer's
steering control to one side. At the same time, she
swiped at the back of Matt's legs with her staff,
flipping him high into the air.

'*Waaaahhhhhh!*'

As Matt, wailing, performed an unexpected
mid-air tumble, the surfer's boom came whipping
across, narrowly missing him. The repositioned
sail billowed out, acting as a brake. Roxie sent the
surfer slewing around into a long side-on skid.

It came to a standstill on the brink of the crevasse – just as Matt landed back on board with a bump.

Roxie's dramatic emergency stop was followed by a long silence. It was broken by the faint *vzzzz-tk* of Matt's Multivision Specs deactivating. Their lenses separated and withdrew behind his temples. Matt tore his gaze from the deadly drop they had just narrowly avoided, and threw Roxie another look.

'*Mind the boom*? What's the rush, Rox?'

Roxie released her hold on the steering control. 'The Sultan's caravan has been attacked, Matt!' she replied. 'By dinosaurs!'

'*Dinosaurs*?'

'I know, right,' said Gomez excitedly. Even he couldn't help finding the prospect of meeting a real live dinosaur thrilling – if also terrifying. Prehistoric beasts were one of the fact-mad Keeper's specialist subjects.

'So – we're checking out Relic Gorge!' Roxie told Matt.

'It's full of dinosaur fossils,' explained Gomez.

Matt looked from one to the other, puzzled.

'I might be having trouble at school,' he said, 'but last I heard, fossils don't attack people.'

Before either Roxie or Gomez could reply, all three friends were startled by a screeching animal cry. They turned to look in the direction from which it had come – and gasped.

'Holy Camoly!' wailed Gomez, paling.

'It's not the *fossils* we need to be worrying about!' cried Roxie.

A high dune rose nearby. Over its crest had just appeared four large green scaly-skinned beasts. They had powerful back legs, thick tails, tiny arms and long, sharp-toothed jaws.

Matt didn't need his dino-mad friend Gomez to tell him what he was looking at . . .

7
Dino Danger

Matt watched in horror as the dinosaur pack came scrambling down the face of the dune, their reptilian eyes fixed on the sand-surfer. He tried to sound calmer than he felt.

'Think you can get this thing up to speed, Rox?'

Roxie was already hurriedly adjusting the position of the surfer's sail.

'You better hope so!'

She tugged on the steering control, coaxing the little craft into life. It took all her skill to harness the light wind. The surfer pulled off along the clifftop, away from the fast-advancing predators. It quickly began to gather speed.

But not quickly enough for Gomez.

'Come *on*!' he wailed. 'Hurry!' His position in the stern meant he was the closest to the pursuing beasts. All four were now sprinting after the surfer. Gomez cried out as one of them, having put on burst of speed, got near enough to take a giant bite out of the hull.

'*Yaaaagh*!'

As the surfer surged forward, the dinosaurs dropped back a metre or two. But within moments, they were gaining once more.

'Lose these things, Roxie!' urged Matt.

Roxie made a decision. If they couldn't outrun the beasts, they would have to outmanoeuvre them.

'Hang on!'

She sent the sand-surfer veering to the right, away from the cliff edge – then yanked hard on the steering control to turn the craft full about. It went zooming flat-out, straight at a banked dune that rose on the very edge of the crevasse.

Before Matt or Gomez had time to scream, the surfer was airborne. It glided across the wide chasm

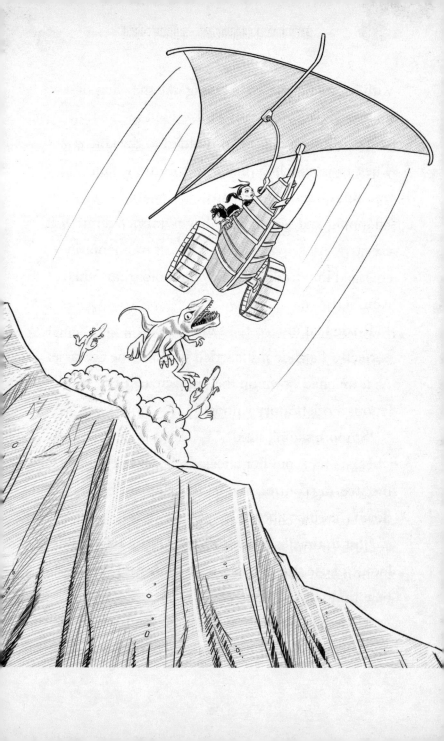

with its sail flat above it, acting like the wing of a hang-glider, keeping it aloft.

The dinosaurs were committed to the chase. They, too, launched themselves from the cliff top. But unlike the sand-surfer, they couldn't fly. Snapping and screeching, they plummeted into the crevasse. As they fell, all four beasts momentarily changed into fizzling blue-white holograms, then vanished.

Roxie had judged the sand-surfer's launch speed perfectly. Its glide just carried it across the crevasse. As it touched down on the opposite clifftop, Matt let out a celebratory whoop.

'Smooth sailin', Rox!'

Roxie blew out her cheeks, relaxed her grip on the steering control, and let the sand-surfer run free down the slope ahead.

'Just in time!' she said, giving Matt a relieved look. 'Those things could have destroyed my beautiful sand-surf . . . er . . . er . . .'

Roxie had just turned her attention back to the way ahead. Her eyes widened with shock.

Her stammering turned into a wild yell.

'. . . er . . . erraaaaAAAAAHHHH!'

Only metres ahead, a giant rock stood directly in the speeding surfer's path. Matt and Gomez saw it too, and added their voices to Roxie's.

'*Aaaaaaaaaahhhhhhhhhhhh!*'

Roxie threw the sand-surfer into another skidding emergency stop.

But this time, it was much too late.

8
The Crumpepper

In the lobby of the Coronet theatre, a little furry figure was pacing the purple carpet like a miniature sentry. Marlon was taking his task of covering for his best friend very seriously. Since Matt's departure, he had been keeping non-stop lookout for the dreaded Mrs Crumpepper.

A rapping on the window of the theatre door made Marlon let out a startled chitter. He looked up to see an elderly woman's face behind the glass.

'*Hello-ho*!'

Before Marlon could take action, Harry Hatter came striding across the lobby to answer the door.

'Hello, Mrs Crumpepper!'

As Harry held the door, a small woman in a mauve skirt, white blouse and large, square-framed spectacles entered the theatre. Her grey hair was fixed in a neat bun. She was carrying an umbrella and a leather briefcase.

'Hello.'

Harry immediately felt like he was ten years old again. It wasn't just the fact that Mrs Crumpepper had once taught him – there was something in the way she had just greeted him, and in the glint in her eye, that made it instantly clear who was in charge.

Marlon had seen enough. With a squeak, he retreated to consider his tactics. Mrs Crumpepper spotted him scampering off. She gave a faint,

'Hmm . . .' and raised an eyebrow – enough to make it clear that she did not approve of free-range exotic pets.

'Sorry to keep you waiting!' said Harry, flustered. 'I was . . . erm . . . looking for Matt! You see, I built this to help with his maths . . .'

He produced a peculiar contraption from behind his back. It was his very latest invention. It looked something like a cross between a giant calculator and an abacus – with a single large lightbulb fixed on top, for good measure.

'The Calcuhelper-3000!' declared Harry proudly.

Mrs Crumpepper gave him a withering look.

'We'll be working with our *brains*!' she said sternly. 'Please put that oversized child's toy away.'

Harry, crestfallen, was glad to see his wife coming across the lobby. He was feeling in need of backup.

'Hello, Mrs Crumpepper!' beamed Meg. 'So nice of you to come at such short notice.'

Matt's mum was strangely fascinated by

Charlotte Crumpepper. On the surface, she seemed
like a prim and proper little old lady – someone
you could imagine enjoying tea from a china pot,
perhaps with a nice English muffin, before getting
back to her knitting. But Meg knew there was
much more to Mrs Crumpepper than met the eye.
This was the woman who had been on numerous
expeditions with Harry's intrepid father, Alfred,
to some of the wildest parts of the globe. Her list
of qualifications included a valid helicopter pilot's
licence and a certificate in Advanced Bushcraft.
She had scheduled Matt's tuition to fit around her
own scuba diving classes. Even now, Meg noticed,
she was wearing wheelie-heels – which were hardly
typical footwear for a pensioner.

'We . . . er . . . sent Matt up to get his books,'
Meg explained awkwardly, 'and . . . erm . . . haven't
seen him since.' She planned to give Matt a piece
of her mind when he showed up. Disappearing was
rude – and embarrassing.

Mrs Crumpepper seemed unworried.

'I can detect a student at 30 metres,' she told

Matt's mum. 'That's 98.4 feet to you Americans!'

Without further comment, she went gliding across the lobby on her wheeled heels, and set off into the theatre to seek her prey.

Meg gazed after her. 'Poor Matt,' she murmured. Despite being cross with her son, she was beginning to wonder what she had let him in for.

'I know,' said Harry absently, still cradling his invention. 'He would have *loved* the Calcuhelper-3000 . . .'

9
Relic Gorge

'Is anyone hurt?'

Matt slowly picked himself up and began brushing the sand from his clothes. Somehow, he was still in one piece.

The crash had been quite something. Colliding with the rock at high speed had smashed the sand-surfer to smithereens, and sent its crew flying. Bits of broken surfer hull, shreds of torn sail and fragments of shattered wheel were scattered all around. The largest piece of wreckage – the surfer's front end, with its skid plate still attached – had ended up on a rocky ledge some distance away.

'*We're OK . . .*' said Roxie, getting to her feet.

She picked up a piece of debris and inspected it miserably. 'But it's game over for my sand-surfer.'

Gomez was the slowest to recover. He was still on his knees, staring woozily at the sand. As his vision cleared, he suddenly came to life.

'Look, guys – *fossils*!'

Half buried in the bank of sand in which Gomez had landed was the fossilized skull of a large, long-jawed beast. Several other fossilized bones lay nearby. As Matt scanned around for more, he took in their surroundings properly for the first time. The surfer had crashed close to the edge of a quarry-like canyon, a vast natural pit that cut deep into the desert terrain.

'Know what, guys?' said Matt. 'I *think* we just found Relic Gorge.'

The three companions hurried to the brink of the

cliff, and gazed down at the sunken expanse of the gorge below. It appeared to be the site of some kind of exploratory dig. Matt could see primitive lifting equipment, wooden packing crates and several areas

where the ground had been carefully excavated.

'This is the place all right,' said Roxie. Her eyes lit up. 'And listen – somebody's busy digging!'

The faint *tink-tink* of metal tapping on stone had just begun to echo around the gorge.

Anticipating their next step, Gomez pulled a face. 'It's a *long* way down,' he said feebly.

The only route to the canyon floor was via a series of rickety-looking timber scaffolds built against the gorge's far wall. Roxie was already figuring out a safe way down them. She drew her staff and began using its tip to sketch a map in the sand at her feet.

'If we use *that* side ramp . . .' she muttered, glancing across the gorge, then drawing some more, '. . . and if *that* ladder's safe, there's another ramp on the – *hey*!'

Roxie's cry of protest had been provoked by Matt wiping out most of her sand diagram – by scooping it up with a wooden bucket.

'Sorry, Rox!' said Matt cheerily. 'Got an idea!'

While Roxie had been busy route-mapping,

Matt had hatched an alternative plan. Only metres away, a wooden platform jutted out from the cliff. Above its end hung a large pulley, supported by timber struts. A rope was threaded through it. One end was tied to a big, open-topped crate that sat near the platform's edge. The other dangled freely. The whole set-up looked like it had been designed for lowering supplies into the canyon.

Matt lugged his sand-filled bucket to the platform and emptied it into the crate. He quickly collected another two bucketfuls. Roxie and Gomez watched, intrigued.

'What are you gonna do?' asked Gomez.

Matt just passed him the free end of the rope. 'Hold this – *very* tight!'

Gomez did as he was told, but not without looking suspicious.

'Why?'

'You'll see.'

'But I don't *wanna* see!'

Ignoring the anxious Keeper, Matt began shoving the sand-filled crate towards the platform's edge.

Roxie watched, puzzled. 'What is this?'

Matt smiled. 'Counterweight.'

Roxie looked blank. 'Counter *what*?'

'The quick way down,' grinned Matt.

A final shove sent the crate plunging into the gorge. Matt quickly grasped the same section of rope as Gomez, and jumped after it – taking the alarmed Keeper with him. Roxie finally saw his plan. She leapt from the platform too, grabbing the rope as she fell.

'*Aaaaaaaaaaaaaaaaaaaaaaaaaaa* . . . !'

As they plummeted into the gorge, Gomez's screaming didn't let up for a moment. The weight of the heavy crate on the rope's other end almost balanced their own. Its pull greatly reduced the speed of their fall, as Matt had intended. But Gomez was still petrified.

'. . . *aaaaaaaaaaaaaaaaaaaaaaaaaaa* . . .!'

The crate whizzed past, on its way back up. They quickly approached the end of their descent.

'Let go . . . *now!*' yelled Matt. Following his lead, Roxie released her grip, dropped to the ground

and sprang clear.

But not Gomez. He clung to the rope like grim death, eyes tight shut. The bump as he hit the ground, on his backside briefly interrupted his screaming. But the fact that his ordeal was over seemed to pass him by. He kept his eyes closed, and resumed his wailing.

'. . . *aaaaaaaaaaaaaaaaaaaaaaaaaa* . . . !'

Matt wondered if yelling helped Gomez deal with things. It had certainly drawn attention to their unexpected arrival – because someone was coming to greet them . . .

10
Doctor Fossil

The man standing over Matt was a peculiar-looking character. It was his wild, wide-eyed stare that Matt noticed first. He had never met anyone with red eyes before.

'Can I help you?'

The stranger's voice had an undertone of manic excitement – as if he was struggling to contain himself. His broad grin made Matt feel uneasy.

'Sure can,' replied Matt, trying to sound confident. 'You can answer some questions.'

'Oh, well, that *is* my life's work!' The man held out his right hand. 'Doctor Fossil, at your service!'

Matt stared at the extended hand. It was

covered by a weird-looking glove, fed by cables that snaked from inside the man's sleeve. It might have belonged to Robo-Enforcer.

Noticing Matt's expression, Doctor Fossil gave

an 'Oh!' of realization. With a look of alarm
that suggested he had just made a major gaffe,
he quickly hid the bizarre glove behind his back
and held out a more normal-looking left hand.
Matt, a little warily, took it and shook it. It felt
cold and clammy.

'Matt Hatter. And these are my friends—'

Matt was cut short by Doctor Fossil's reaction
to hearing his name. 'Soooo!' he breathed,
yanking Matt so close that their faces almost
touched. His red eyes goggled as he pumped
Matt's hand up and down. 'I finally meet the
famous Matt Hatter!'

Matt, unnerved, tugged his hand free and
stepped back.

'And the almost as famous Gomez!' chirped
Gomez, approaching.

Roxie gave Gomez a withering look, then
addressed Doctor Fossil herself. 'You, erm,
mentioned your life's work . . .'

'Yeah,' said Matt. 'What kind of work would
that be?'

'Why, palaeontology!' replied Doctor Fossil, as though it was the *only* kind. 'The study of prehistoric fossils!' He turned away, beckoning them to follow him. 'You *must* see some of these amazing specimens!'

'I must, I MUST!' agreed Gomez. 'I *love* fossils!'

He set off eagerly after the Doctor. Roxie made as if to follow, then hesitated. She picked up something from the ground. Looking rather forlorn, she showed it Matt.

'It's a piece of my surfer . . .'

There was a dinosaur-sized bite missing from the fragment of sand-surfer hull. Matt gave his friend a consoling look. They both hurried after Gomez.

Doctor Fossil led them across the site and up a rickety wooden ramp on to a higher shelf of rock. Here, a number of makeshift tables held dozens of fossil specimens. Gomez's eyes gleamed.

Roxie, however, had other priorities. 'Very nice, Doc,' she said impatiently, 'but *we're* interested in *living* dinosaurs.'

Doctor Fossil gave a condescending chuckle.

'None of those here, my dear! Only the fossilized remains of those extinct, noble beasts!'

'*Noble*?' scowled Matt. He took the piece of wreckage from Roxie and held it up. 'How noble is taking a bite out of our sand-surfer? We just got attacked by a vicious bunch of chomping dinosaurs!'

Gomez was keen to show off his knowledge in front of a real palaeontologist. He wagged a finger at Matt. 'Uh-uh. Early theropods,' he corrected him. 'Eoraptors.'

Doctor Fossil laughed again. '*Attacked by theropods*? Preposterous!' he cried. 'They've been extinct for millions of years!' He gave Matt a pitying look. 'Only a *fool* would ever suggest such nonsense!'

'He's been having trouble at school lately,' Gomez explained, a little smugly.

'Oh, *thanks*, Gomez!' said Matt, looking peeved. He was used to his Keeper friend being a bit of a geek – but he wasn't usually so tactless.

Gomez, however, had only one thing on his mind.

'Were there any *particular* fossils you wanted to show us, Doctor?'

Doctor Fossil beamed. 'Ah-ha, a curious lad! Here, *look*!' He proudly presented one of the larger specimens to Gomez.

'Oooh! A trilobite!'

'Exactly!'

Doctor Fossil selected another specimen for Gomez to admire and identify. But Matt had already seen enough. He decided to leave the pair of fossil-fanatics to it. He turned and walked away – and was glad when Roxie followed. Together they jumped back down on to the lower level of the site.

'I didn't bail on my homework and come to another dimension for more lessons!' grumbled Matt, once Doctor Fossil and Gomez were out of earshot. 'Let's take a look around, Rox . . .'

They made their way over to a large canvas tent, which Matt guessed provided Doctor Fossil's living quarters. There were a number of crates stacked to one side of it. Roxie went to take a closer look at them.

But something else had caught Matt's attention.

'Hey . . . *nice* set of wheels!'

A green and orange dune buggy was parked in front of the tent. It had a bucket seat for the driver, full suspension, high-grip tyres and a cool rear spoiler. It was powered by a caged propeller at the back, like a giant fan.

'Now, *this* is how to travel in the Sea of Sands,' enthused Matt.

Roxie had found an open crate, and was peering inside. She looked up to speak to Matt.

'Don't you think there's something suspicious about that Doctor Fossil?'

Matt was busy admiring the buggy's interior. He shrugged. 'He's annoying, for sure – but I don't get the feeling he's our thief.'

Roxie turned her attention back to the crate. She let out a gasp.

'*Isn't* he?'

She pulled a silver scimitar with a jewelled hilt from inside the crate. There was a large chunk missing from its curving blade.

'This has to be Captain Yasser's sword!' said Roxie. 'He told me and Gomez that a dinosaur snatched it from him during the attack on the camel caravan! Check the bite marks . . .'

She held the sword blade against the piece of surfer wreckage.

'They match!' cried Matt.

'And if this *is* Yasser's,' Roxie went on, 'I'll bet all these crates are from the Sultan's shipment.

So what are they doing on Fossil's dig site, huh?'

Matt had to agree that Roxie's suspicions seemed justified. It looked like Doctor Fossil might not be the innocent scientist he claimed to be.

And they had just left Gomez alone with him . . .

11
A Villain Unveiled

Doctor Fossil held a cruelly curved Velociraptor claw high over his head. 'And see how the claw is as sharp as a knife!' he told Gomez, who was watching him, fascinated. 'For ripping and gutting its prey!'

A wild glint flashed in the scientist's eyes. It looked almost as though he was about to bring the claw slashing down . . .

'Gomez! LOOK OUT!'

Matt swooped from nowhere, swinging on the dangling hook of one of the site's makeshift cranes. He planted a double-footed kick on Doctor Fossil's raised arm. Fossil let out a howl,

and the claw went flying.

'Ooowwwr!'

Matt landed in a crouch beside Gomez.

'Saved you!'

But Gomez didn't seem to think he had
been in need of saving. He hurried to the aid

of Doctor Fossil, who was nursing his wrist.

'What's *wrong* with you, Matt?' he scowled.
'Do you treat *all* your teachers like this?'

Matt was running out of patience.

'Newsflash, Einstein,' he snapped at Gomez.
'Your good Doctor Fossil, yeah, *he's* behind the dino attacks!'

Roxie joined Matt. She held up the bitten scimitar and surfer fragment for Gomez to see.

'If the bite fits . . .' she said.

Matt glared accusingly at Doctor Fossil.
'Admit it, Doc – it's you behind the attacks!'

Doctor Fossil's injured expression slowly turned to a look of menace. His red eyes seemed to flash.

'You may not be here to learn . . .' he muttered, glaring at Matt. Without warning, he grabbed the front of Gomez's tunic with his gloved hand,
'. . . but you still need a lesson or two!'

With astonishing ease, Fossil lifted the startled Keeper from the ground and flung him through the air.

'Aaaaaahhh!'

Gomez, wailing, collided with Matt and Roxie, bowling them over.

With a roar, Doctor Fossil threw back his arms and head. His military shirt disappeared. Matt was shocked to see that the scientist's exposed upper body was inhumanly lean and scrawny, and covered in lumpy ridged reptilian skin. A sphere of glowing amber, encircled by steel, was set deep in Fossil's chest.

The three friends watched in horror as streams of crackling energy began

to pour from Fossil's out-thrust chest. Like curving
forks of lightning, they converged on the centre
of the nearby excavation, where the fossilized
dinosaur skeleton lay. As suddenly as they had
begun, the energy streams cut out. A moment later,
four living Eoraptors, like the ones that had chased
the sand-surfer, emerged from the pit.

Doctor Fossil greeted the appearance of the
reanimated dinosaurs with a wild laugh. He lifted
his gloved hand, holding it as if it were the head of
a creature and his forearm its neck. As he twisted
and flexed his glove, all four dinosaurs mimicked
its movements exactly.

'That's it!' raved Fossil. 'Dance, my beauties!'

Laughing madly, he broke into a funky disco-
style dance, feet shuffling, knees knocking, hips
swivelling. Every groovy move he made was
copied precisely by all four Eoraptors.

'The Doc's controlling those dinos like puppets!'
cried Gomez.

Matt and Roxie, getting to their feet, watched
the dancing dinosaurs in disbelief. It would have

been funny – if it wasn't terrifying.

'I could say you're right,' said Matt, helping Gomez up. 'But I'd rather say – RUN!'

As the three friends fled, Doctor Fossil stopped dancing and twisted his gloved hand in their direction. All four Eoraptors obediently turned their heads. Fossil let out another wild laugh.

'Yes, run!' he cried, as he sent his pack of predators after their prey. 'But we're gonna getcha . . .!'

12

A Surprise in Store

Mrs Crumpepper's eyesight wasn't what it once had been – but with her spectacles on, she still knew a skateboard trail when she saw one.

Keeping her eyes on the carpet and a firm grip on her umbrella and briefcase, she wheelie-heeled her way gracefully along the corridor. The skater trail came to an end outside a door marked 'PRIVATE'. Mrs Crumpepper put her things down beside the wall, opened the door and peered inside.

The cluttered storeroom was unoccupied, but from the faint smell of warm dust, Mrs Crumpepper guessed its light had been

on only recently.
She switched it on
again now – and
immediately noticed
the open cardboard
box that sat in a
cleared space on
the floor.

*That young man
was in here not long ago,
I'll be bound,* thought
Mrs Crumpepper.
She went to
take a closer look
at the open box – and let out a gasp of surprise.
Memories flashed before her mind's eye. She
had helped Alfred Hatter pack away these film
cans herself – many years ago, when they were
childhood friends. They had been helping Alfred's
father, Samuel Hatter, on the fateful day on which
he announced he was closing down Screen Two.
At the time, neither she nor Alfred had known the

reason. It was only later, when Alfred took over the running of the Coronet, that Samuel Hatter had shared his remarkable secret with his son – and years later still before Alfred had confided in Charlotte Crumpepper.

She could still recall that strange conversation, during the final leg of their two-person expedition to Angel Falls. It was only because it had been Alfred that she'd believed a word of it.

Mrs Crumpepper chuckled to herself. It was funny to think that her dear old friend's grandson should be tied up with such everyday concerns as schoolwork. The boy had no idea of the huge responsibility he would one day inherit.

Just you wait, young Matthew Hatter . . .

Thoughts of her student brought Mrs Crumpepper back to the present.

I must get on with tracking that young scallywag down.

In her time, she had trailed everything from snow leopards to salamanders. She wasn't about to let a thirteen-year-old boy give her the slip.

As she went to switch off the storeroom light,

Mrs Crumpepper thought she caught a glimpse of movement amid the clutter.

No. Just my old eyes playing up again.

She closed the door behind her. Retrieving her umbrella and briefcase, she noticed that the briefcase had come unfastened. Once it was safely rebuckled, she scooted off to continue her search for Matt.

In the dark, silent storeroom, a pair of eyes shone brightly. Marlon, crouching beneath a pile of junk, breathed a sigh of relief. He looked at the sheaf of papers he had managed to snatch from Mrs Crumpepper's briefcase – her home tuition worksheets – and chittered cheerfully. Phase One of Operation Crumpepper had gone smoothly. Marlon hoped that swiping the old lady's notes would buy Matt some time. Now he just had to dispose of the evidence.

With another sigh, the little Tasmanian devil tore off a scrap of worksheet, shoved it in his mouth and began to chew. He swallowed, belched loudly, then pulled a face. Maths even *tasted* horrible.

13

Eoraptor Scrap

Mrs Crumpepper wasn't the only one on Matt's trail. Far away, in another dimension, a pack of four ferocious dinosaurs were after him. He, Roxie and Gomez were running for their lives across Relic Gorge, with Doctor Fossil's reanimated Eoraptors snapping at their heels.

Running away came naturally to Gomez. But it wasn't Roxie's style. She preferred to stand her ground. Even as she ran, she was preparing to defend herself. She reached over her shoulder for her staff, and swiftly extended it to its full length.

The lead Eoraptor pounced – but Roxie was ready for it. She leapt high, twirled around and brought her staff whipping through the air.

'Take *that*!'

As Roxie's staff blow struck the Eoraptor, it changed from a creature of solid flesh to a flickering, translucent blue hologram. A moment later, it disappeared.

With the speed of a ninja, Roxie took a fierce swipe at a second dinosaur. Like the first,

it turned into a hologram, then vanished.

Matt, too, was putting up a fight. As the dinosaur tailing him sprang, he made a last minute dive for a shovel lying nearby. He grabbed it, forward-rolled and came up facing his leaping attacker. A mighty whack from the shovel made the Eoraptor dematerialize in mid-air.

Gomez was faring less well. The fourth dinosaur

had cornered him against a stack of packing crates. The terrified Keeper was trying, rather feebly, to fend it off with a broom.

'Shoo! Go away! Shoo!'

The Eoraptor swallowed the head of the broom in one monster bite.

'Aargh!'

Gomez, paralysed with fear, clutched one end of the broom handle helplessly as the dinosaur quickly munched its way along it from the other. Having devoured Gomez's only method of defence, it pounced . . .

. . . and dissolved into thin air as Matt, coming to the rescue in the nick of time, clobbered it hard with his shovel.

'Bullseye!' grinned Matt. A moment later, however, his smile, like the dinosaur, had vanished.

Doctor Fossil was spectating from the platform of rock on which his specimen tables stood. He was clearly having fun.

'Fools!' he shrieked, red eyes gleaming. 'I've got more!'

Once again, he flung out his arms and threw back his head. Crackling streams of white energy burst from his chest. Moments later, four more live Eoraptors sprang from the excavation pit.

With a theatrical gesture of his gloved hand, Doctor Fossil sent the reanimated dinosaurs after Matt, Gomez and Roxie.

'C'mon!' yelled Matt. 'The buggy!'

He sprinted over to the dune buggy, leapt into the driver's seat and hit the ignition. The vehicle's giant propeller whirred into life. As Roxie and Gomez piled into the back seats, Matt took a firm grip on the steering wheel, and floored the accelerator. The buggy shot forward, the blast from its propeller spraying dust and sand at the advancing dinosaurs.

Swerving round rocks and specimen crates, Matt drove flat out towards a gap in the gorge's high rock wall. The dune buggy hurtled into a narrow crevasse, with Matt clinging grimly to its controls.

'We're not losing them!' wailed Gomez.

Matt glanced anxiously in his wing mirror. The chasing Eoraptors were only metres behind.

'Man, those critters are fast!'

'Too bad it's not dark,' moaned Gomez. 'They have terrible night vision.'

Matt's face lit up. 'Good idea, Gomez!'

Gomez looked blank. 'What idea?'

By way of reply, Matt slammed the steering wheel hard to the left. The buggy skidded round, till it was facing the crevasse's rock wall. Directly ahead was the boarded-up entrance of an old mining tunnel. As Matt headed straight for it at full speed, both Roxie and Gomez cried out.

'*Whoa*!'

The buggy smashed through the rotten planks and went bouncing wildly along the unlit tunnel beyond. Gomez, glancing back, gave a cry of delight.

'Look – they're afraid of the dark!'

The four Eoraptors had come to a halt at the mouth of the tunnel. They were chirruping and screeching in protest, clearly unwilling to enter the

dingy passage, where their eyesight would fail.

Smiling, Matt eased off on the speed. For now, at least, they were out of danger. He flicked on the buggy's headlamps, and concentrated on the route ahead.

14

A Trap is Set

'How will you stop them, My Lord?' squeaked Craw.

The little gargoyle hung in the air beside Tenoroc, flapping his tiny wings frantically. He had been following the action in Relic Gorge, relayed in the glimmering orb of the Triple Sphere, over Tenoroc's shoulder. He was eagerly awaiting his master's next move.

Discovering that Matt Hatter was once again in play in the Multiverse and meddling in his schemes, had driven Tenoroc into a wild fury. Craw, however, liked nothing better than watching his master take on a Hatter Hero. There was little other entertainment in the dreary dead-end dimension of the Sky Prison.

'With a little *twist*, Craw,' hissed Tenoroc, smiling sinisterly. He raised a hand, and a small hexagonal disc floated up into his underling's view. With a twirl of one long bony finger, Tenoroc set it spinning where it hovered.

Craw giggled with wicked delight. The silver-edged disc was one of Tenoroc's Spatter Traps. They were always a treat . . .

Tenoroc's Traps relied on his ability to manipulate space and matter. He had the power to create a bubble of unreality, concealed within normal reality. Once inside a Trap, Tenoroc's prey would face hazards invisible to the naked eye, including creatures as weird and wonderful – and deadly – as Tenoroc's evil imagination could produce.

Tenoroc would have given anything to deal with the Hatter boy in person. But as long as he was trapped in the Sky Prison, that was not to be.

He consoled himself with the thought that watching his young enemy perish in a Trap would be the next best thing.

He lowered the floating Trap disc into the socket in the top of the Triple Sphere. The disc flared with light. The trio of spikes at each end of the Sphere swung together to form a point. Slowly, the entire device began to turn, like a top.

Still giggling with anticipation, Craw plonked himself down on the table beside the Triple Sphere. As it spun faster, he began a funny little dance around it.

'Ha, ha, ha . . . tee, hee, hee!' tittered the gargoyle, twirling about.

Cloudbursts of red and blue energy exploded in the Triple Sphere's upper and lower orbs. As the colours trickled into the central orb and combined, the Sphere spun faster still. It began to spiral around the rock table on which it stood – and collided with the giddy, prancing Craw. With a squeal of dismay, the gargoyle went flying.

Tenoroc ignored his unlucky underling. His eyes were fixed on the Triple Sphere's eerie glare. With another wicked grin, he snarled the command that would activate the Trap.

'Shifting space and matter . . .'

15
The Hornets' Nest

As he drove the dune buggy further along the mining tunnel, Matt had no idea what might lie in the darkness ahead. But giant sunflowers were certainly a surprise.

'*Weird*!' said Roxie, as the buggy's headlamps lit the big yellow-and-brown blooms lining both sides of the passage.

'Flowers don't grow in the dark . . .' said Gomez.

Matt was quickest to see the only explanation.

'Spatter Trap!' he cried. 'It's Tenoroc!'

Even from his prison, Tenoroc had the ability to manipulate space and matter. Thanks to his weakened powers, however, his Traps weren't always

perfectly concealed. A telltale glitch – such as the improbable sunflowers – was a sure sign he had been messing with reality.

And if Tenoroc had created a Trap, there was only one way Matt was going to find a way through it. He needed to see the hidden dimension.

'Going Multivision!'

As Matt gave the activation command, the Multivision Specs wiped back over his eyes. His view dissolved in a twisting swirl of colours, and was replaced by a true view of the Trap terrain.

'Hang on!' cried Matt, as the buggy suddenly dropped, then bounced wildly. He fought to keep control. 'Whoa! What is this place?'

The buggy was moving along a wide brown tunnel. Its floor and walls included patches of yellow, made up of interlocking hexagonal cells, so thin they were translucent. Matt steered around some, worried that they wouldn't hold the buggy's weight – then swerved the other way to avoid a stream of golden goop dribbling from above. The sticky goo – was it honey? – was leaking

from lots of places along the tunnel's ceiling.

'L-Looks like a giant wasp's nest!' said Gomez nervously.

Matt spotted something up ahead, approaching fast.

'Incoming!'

A huge flying creature, with a yellow-and-black segmented body and transparent wings, was zooming towards them. As it approached, a second creature came into view further along the tunnel, then a third.

'They're *massive*!' cried Matt. 'And what kind of wasp has a scaly head like that?'

As the first of the creatures drew near, it suddenly became visible to Roxie and Gomez, too.

'Dragon Hornets!' yelled Gomez, terrified.

Then the Hornet was upon them. It made a grab for the dune buggy's roof-bars with its six multi-jointed legs, but Matt managed to steer clear. He dodged the second Hornet, too. But as he concentrated on avoiding a downpour of goop, the third giant insect swooped.

'Maaaaatttt!'

Roxie and Gomez cried out as the buggy was lifted clear of the tunnel's floor. There was nothing Matt could do.

'Rox!' he yelled. 'Swat that bug!'

The feisty Tracker sprang into action. She drew her staff, extended it and took a fierce swipe at the Hornet's armoured head. The blow was enough to make the creature release its grip. The dune buggy tumbled through the air in a stomach-churning somersault.

'Aaaaaaahhhhh!'

As the buggy's wheels slammed back on to the tunnel floor, Matt managed to regain control just in time to dodge the next hazard. More Dragon Hornets came swooping past.

'Matt – get us *outta* here!' cried Roxie.

Matt didn't need telling. The sooner they were clear of this multi-dimensional mayhem, the better. And something he half-remembered about wasps' nests had just flashed across his mind.

'If my hunch is right,' he muttered, 'this nest

is made of *paper*!'

   There was only one way to test his theory. As a dead end loomed up ahead, Matt floored the buggy's accelerator, and headed straight for it . . .

16
An Empty Cell

One moment the rock wall of the crevasse looked as solid as . . . well . . . rock. The next, part of it began to ripple and stretch, like a thick-skinned bubble.

The dune buggy burst from Tenoroc's hidden Trap, back into normal space. It landed on the rocky ground, and skidded to a halt. Matt's plan to bust out of the Dragon Hornets' paper nest had worked.

Roxie, in her back seat, pulled a face as she plucked bits of honeycombed nest wall from her clothing.

'Yuk! Who's smart idea was the detour?'

Gomez looked defensive. 'At least we lost the 'raptors!'

'Let's hope we didn't lose Fossil,' said Matt, frowning. 'Now we know the double-crossing Doc is in league with Tenoroc, his days are numbered. I'm taking him down, for Grandpa's sake . . .'

Matt's quest to clean up the Multiverse was driven by his determination to free his grandfather, Alfred Hatter, from the prison dimension in which he was trapped. To do so meant capturing the Super Villains Tenoroc still had under his control. By locking them away in the Villain Vault – a unique prison dimension contained within *The Interactive Chronicles of Action and Adventure* – Matt could shift the balance of power between Tenoroc and his grandfather, in Alfred's favour. If he could lock them *all* away, Matt hoped he could give his grandfather enough strength to break free.

'How does that creep do it, anyway?' asked Roxie. 'Bring dinos back to life, I mean?'

Matt reached into his backpack and pulled out the *Chronicles*. As he opened the book, light blazed from within it. As always, its spread pages automatically displayed the exact content Matt wanted to view – in this instance, the Villain Vault. The left-hand page showed a movie poster for *Doctor Fossil*. The barred Vault cell on the opposite page was empty.

'At least we know where he came from,' murmured Matt. 'Aha! Here we go . . . it says here that Fossil's amber heart gives him the ability to reanimate dead creatures . . .'

'And we're talking *long* dead!' put in Roxie.

'. . . and that his unique cyber-glove has the power to fire blasts of explosive energy and exert superhuman force.'

'Sounds familiar,' said Gomez, rubbing his chest.

'Anything about how to take him down?' asked Roxie.

'Nope, 'fraid not.' Matt slammed the *Chronicles* shut. His Multivision Specs deactivated. 'My guess is we need to put that amber heart of his out of operation.'

'So, Matt,' smirked Roxie. 'Think you can be a heartbreaker as well as a Hatter Hero?'

'You bet!' replied Matt, slipping the *Chronicles* back into his pack. He fired up the dune buggy again, and took a determined hold on the steering wheel. 'Let's go Fossil hunting . . .'

17
Marlon's Plan

'**M***atthew Ha-tter!*'

Mrs Crumpepper's search for her
reluctant student had brought her to his lair
– Matt's bedroom, on the Coronet's top floor.
As she sang out his name, her beady eyes
roamed the turret room for signs of life.

Marlon, meanwhile, was doing his very best to
throw Mrs Crumpepper off the scent. The little
Tasmanian devil was on the floor below, in the
family bathroom, where he was struggling to put
a cunning diversion plan into practice.

The first setback had been his discovery that
the toilet bowl was impossible to climb. Its smooth

overhanging sides offered no grip for his tiny paws. After several failed attempts, Marlon had come up with an alternative strategy. Using the bathroom scales as a springboard, he had managed to trampoline on to the top of the bowl. Things had nearly taken a nasty turn when an awkward landing on the toilet seat almost sent him toppling into the bowl. He had regained his balance just in time.

Now, having inched his way around the slippery plastic seat and bravely scaled the cistern pipe, he was within reach of his goal – the dangling handle of the flush chain. Marlon took a deep breath. It was quite a leap for a little rodent, particularly one with a tummy full of worksheets. But he wasn't about to let Matt down.

He launched himself at the chain-pull, and wrapped his furry arms around it. Clinging on bravely, he jiggled about, trying to maximize the tug of his slight weight. He gave a triumphant chitter as, at last, the chain-pull began to descend.

The *fwrwooooooshhh* of the toilet flushing carried

to the bedroom above. As she heard the telltale sound, Mrs Crumpepper's eyes lit up.

'Aha!' she cried. 'Got you!'

She hurried for the stairs, planning to lie in wait for her prey outside the bathroom door.

18

The Battle of the Gorge

Doctor Fossil was confident that he had seen the last of Matt Hatter. He was free now to resume his mission for Lord Tenoroc – to find and reanimate the ultimate demon beast. Then, once Tenoroc was satisfied, he could return to his own research. The Sultan's stolen riches would provide generous funds to support his scientific quest for unlimited power. With an army of resurrected dinosaurs at his command, he would rule the world of chaos that Tenoroc was so determined to create . . .

The crazed palaeontologist cast his eyes eagerly over part of Relic Gorge's high rock wall.

'Oh, the *thrill* of exploration . . .'

He raised his gloved right hand and pointed it at the rock face, grinning.

'. . . and blowing things up!'

Streams of energy shot from the cyber-glove's bulging fingertips. As they struck, the rock exploded. Doctor Fossil's wild laughter was drowned out by the crash of falling rubble.

Then, as the dust cloud from the rockfall slowly cleared, Fossil saw something that wiped the grin from his face.

'*YOU!*'

Matt, Roxie and Gomez stood only metres away. Roxie had her staff in hand. All three were poised to attack.

'That's right!' growled Matt. 'Tenoroc's traps can't stop us!'

Fossil glared back, livid. 'This time, Hatter, I'll teach you a *real* lesson!'

'Actually, Doc, I'm here to school you,' replied Matt coolly. He exchanged looks with Roxie and Gomez. 'Or, should I say, we are.'

Even Gomez was ready for a fight. Not many things got the timid Keeper fired up enough to take someone on. But he had trusted Fossil as a fellow lover of science. 'Dirty, stinkin' villain!' he muttered, giving Fossil his meanest stare.

As one, the friends pounced. Together, they managed to pin the villainous scientist to the ground.

'You got me, kids!' wailed Fossil. 'You've really got me . . .' His red eyes flashed, '. . . *ANGRY!*'

Using the power of his energized glove, Fossil effortlessly threw off all three of his attackers. As Matt, Roxie and Gomez went flying, he sprang back to his feet, laughing once more.

The friends picked themselves up, and bravely confronted their enemy again. 'Give up, Fossil!' demanded Matt. 'It's three to one.'

'True,' Doctor Fossil smiled his sweetest smile. 'But as I recall, only *one* of us has an amber heart!'

Without warning, he unleashed another blast from his cyber-glove. Matt dived out of its path – just in time. A boulder right next to him exploded, showering him with debris.

Doctor Fossil let loose another blast, and then another. As crackling bolts of energy came fizzing their way, Matt, Roxie and Gomez did everything they could to dodge them.

'Bravo!' cried Fossil, as a series of near misses sent the three friends scurrying desperately back and forth. 'I *love* your sporty spirit . . .'

He fired his cyber-glove again.

This time, the blast caused a large section of cliff to collapse. As an avalanche of boulders came rumbling down over Matt, Roxie and Gomez, Fossil's laughter grew ever wilder.

'*So* much fun!'

Then, suddenly, he fell silent. His eyes widened, and his gloved hand fell to his side. He stared at the rock face that his last blast had exposed.

'It . . . it can't be . . .' he whispered in awe. 'I've . . . I've *found* it . . . I've FOUND IT!' His voice rose to a jubilant cry. 'Oh, *AMAZING*!'

Matt, Gomez and Roxie had all somehow survived the rockfall. They scrambled to the top of the pile of rubble, hoping to get out of harm's way. From there, Matt followed Doctor Fossil's gaze, to see what it was that had mesmerized the scientist.

'What is *that*?'

A huge fossilized dinosaur skeleton, many times the size of the excavated Eoraptor, was visible in the face of the cliff.

'It's a . . . it's a . . .' Gomez began – then

admitted defeat. 'I have *no* idea!'

Doctor Fossil, however, knew exactly what he had found.

'It's the ultimate demon beast!' he cried ecstatically. 'A complete fossil of Terrorsaurus Rexus Rex!' His red eyes met Matt's, and flashed with triumph. 'Too late, young Hatter . . .'

Fossil's amber heart began to glow more brightly – and Matt realized, with horror, what he was about to do.

'NO! *Stop*!'

But Doctor Fossil was right. Matt was too late.

19

The Demon Beast

Streams of white-hot energy burst from Doctor Fossil's amber heart to strike the giant dinosaur skeleton. Before Matt's horrified gaze, the fossilized bones transformed into a living beast. It tore itself from the rock face and stomped down to the floor of the gorge, making the ground tremble. Opening its awesome jaws, it let out a mighty roar.

Several of Matt's favourite movies featured a good old T-Rex or two. They were pretty big and scary. But Terrorsaurus Rexus Rex was in a different league – bigger and scarier by far. And what made this one scarier still was that it was under the control of Doctor Fossil.

'Go, my prehistoric friend!' cried Fossil. He lifted and thrust forward his cyber-gloved hand.

As the giant dinosaur came straight for him, Matt snatched up a piece of wooden scaffold from among the rubble. The Terrorsaurus lunged. Matt leapt from the rubble pile and thrust the thick wooden strut into its gaping mouth.

'Chew on that, Dino-breath!'

Matt landed close to one of the beast's massive clawed feet. He looked up in satisfaction at his handiwork. The furious dinosaur was struggling to close its jaws, wedged open by the wooden strut.

A moment later, however, Matt's smile faded. The strut had given way. With another roar, the Terrorsaurus attacked again. Its jaws snapped shut over the space Matt had occupied only a split second earlier.

Matt sprinted away across the gorge. His giant foe, urged on by Doctor Fossil, lumbered after him. The chase was on.

The Terrorsaurus had the advantage that it could cover more ground in one earth-shaking

stride than Matt could in ten. But Matt had a few tricks up his sleeve. In the Multiverse, the way gravity worked meant that Matt's strength, speed and agility were all greatly enhanced. He could do things as Hatter Hero that he couldn't dream of as a schoolboy. Springing, leaping and tumbling around the dig site like an acrobat, he narrowly managed to avoid being gobbled up.

Then, finally, it seemed lie his number was up. He found himself backed against a stack of large boulders, with the Terrorsaurus looming over him. Doctor Fossil, laughing wildly, made the giant beast rear its head, ready for a final attack . . .

'Whoa!'

Matt let out a cry of surprise as someone grabbed his ankles from behind. His legs were whipped from under him. Before the dinosaur could strike, he was dragged backwards through a small gap in the rocks.

The someone was Roxie. She and Gomez had found a tiny cave-like shelter among the boulders. Matt had no time to thank her for saving him before the Terrorsaurus's massive head came crashing against the rock pile. Doctor Fossil, it seemed, was going to dig them out.

The three friends looked out miserably through the gap in the rocks at the Terrorsaurus's huge, drooling jaws.

'You still like dinosaurs, Gomez?' asked Roxie.

'Not so much,' replied Gomez feebly.

The Terrorsaurus's head withdrew, then came crashing in once more.

Roxie anxiously watched the boulders around her shake and shift. 'This isn't *exactly* how I pictured our day ending . . .'

Matt, meanwhile, was thinking hard. Unless they could come up with a plan – and fast – there was a very real chance that Trackers, Keepers and Hatter Heroes were all about to go extinct.

20

Gomez to the Rescue

Doctor Fossil was delighted with the way things were turning out.

'How pleased Tenoroc will be!' he crowed. 'Matt Hatter, destroyed by his dark lordship's own demon beast!' With a thrust of his cyber-glove, he made the Terrorsaurus ram the boulder pile again. 'That's it! Dance to the power of my amber heart!'

Matt, crouching under the rocks, had finally had an idea.

'A landslide unleashed this monster,' he muttered to himself. 'Maybe a landslide can stop it . . .'

He looked at Roxie and Gomez, his eyes shining with new hope. 'You guys – divert Slobberchops!'

Seeing Matt's look, Roxie perked up. 'OK,' she said, 'I'll try!' She moved to the opening and unsheathed her staff. Yelling out at the

Terrorsaurus, she flung the staff right past it.

'Go fetch!'

For a moment, the dinosaur's instincts overrode Fossil's control. It turned its massive head to follow the flight of Roxie's staff. By the time it turned back, Matt had slipped away.

Roxie, too, broke cover. She was determined to keep the Terrorsaurus occupied while Matt did whatever it was he was planning to do. Before the dinosaur could react, she had sprung on to the back of its neck, and grabbed hold of one of its long rigid spines.

'Gotcha!'

Doctor Fossil watched, furious. 'Stupid girl!' he cried. 'Off! Shoo!'

He began throwing his gloved hand up, down, back and forth. The Terrorsaurus thrashed around like a bucking bronco. Roxie, wailing, clung on for dear life.

'*Waaaaaahhhh*!'

Gomez, meanwhile, had yet to leave the shelter of the boulder pile.

'I'll . . . er . . . stay here,' he told no one in particular. 'And look after . . .' he looked around his hiding place sheepishly, '. . . erm . . . me!'

Roxie's dinosaur rodeo ride suddenly took a turn for the worse. As the Terrorsaurus shook its head violently, she lost her grip. She went sailing through the air, landed heavily and lay still. Doctor Fossil, laughing wildly, sent the Terrorsaurus lumbering her way.

'Ha-ha, it's *stomping* time!'

Despite his instinct for self-preservation, Gomez was not about to watch his best friend get squashed. He burst from his hiding place and sprinted to her aid.

'*Roxie*!'

The young Keeper's heroics only increased Fossil's delight. He made the Terrorsaurus lift one of its massive feet. 'Two ants, crushed in one stroke!' he cried gleefully. '*So* efficient!'

But at that moment, a voice called out from behind him.

'Hey! Fossil Face! Over here!'

Fossil turned. 'Matt Hatter!' he shrieked, eyes blazing. He thrust his gloved hand in Matt's direction. *'Get him!'*

The Terrorsaurus obediently turned and stomped off towards where Matt stood, at the foot of the gorge wall. Gomez grabbed his chance to grab Roxie. He quickly dragged her to safety.

Matt, meanwhile – now that he had Fossil's attention – was hurriedly scaling the gorge wall, using every bit of his Multiverse-boosted agility. He swung and leapt from one narrow ledge to another, like a monkey, until he was dangling from an overhang at roughly the Terrorsaurus's head height. He hung there, completely vulnerable, tempting the dinosaur to attack.

'C'mon . . .'

Doctor Fossil thrust his cyber-glove forward. The Terrorsaurus butted its armoured head against the rock face with ferocious force. Matt swung clear just in time.

As the dinosaur drew back, Matt could see – and hear – that thin cracks were spreading across the rock face. His plan was working. He swung back to dangle from the overhang once more.

'C'mon . . .' he muttered under his breath. 'Give me *one* more!'

Doctor Fossil was too desperate to crush Matt to realize what was about to happen. He commanded the Terrorsaurus to ram the cliff again. Matt, once more, swung clear at the last moment. He settled on a high ledge, out of harm's way.

This time, the impact of the dinosaur's charge brought the entire overhang crashing down. The Terrorsaurus was buried under an avalanche of falling rock. The crushing force was too much even for a monster of its size and strength to endure.

Doctor Fossil let out a wail of anguish as the giant body of his beloved Terrorsaurus Rexus Rex flickered holographic blue, then vanished.

21
A Broken Heart

Up on the high ledge, Matt had avoided being caught in the overhang's collapse. It was the same ledge, in fact, on which part of the front end of Roxie's wrecked sand-surfer had ended up, after the crash. Seeing it now, with its skid still intact, gave Matt an idea.

'One last ride for the surfer!' he cried, jumping into what remained of the little craft's prow. As he urged it forward, off the ledge, his Multivision Specs activated – *vzzz-tk*!

Doctor Fossil watched in astonishment and dismay as Matt, in his makeshift ride, came hurtling down the slope of rubble created by the rockfall,

straight towards him.

'And, to quote Roxie,' yelled Matt cheerily,
'*mind the boom!*'

As he shot past Fossil, Matt swung out the
surviving part of the sand-surfer's sturdy boom.
It caught the stunned villain squarely across the

chest – a direct hit on his glowing amber heart.
With a violent discharge of energy, the gemstone
split right across its centre. The blow sent Fossil
sprawling backwards, wailing, red eyes wide
with shock. He landed flat on his back in the
Eoraptor pit.

Matt sprang from the surfer to finish the job.
He quickly slipped the *Chronicles* from his backpack,
and reached for his Cell Blaster, slung beneath it.

'Argghh!' yowled Doctor Fossil, clutching at his
cracked amber heart. Its steady glow had become a

weak flicker. '*Arrgggggghhhh*!' Now Fossil's entire body began to flicker, appearing solid one moment, then translucent blue the next.

'Going hologram won't help you, Fossil!' cried Matt. He grasped the Cell Blaster's grip, and felt its DNA-lock kick in. The Blaster fired up, thrumming and glowing with amber light. Matt pointed its hexagonal end at Doctor Fossil, and hit the trigger.

'NOOOOOOO!'

Fossil let out a desperate cry as a writhing stream of dazzling energy burst from the Cell Blaster and

latched on to him. Matt fought to keep the bucking Blaster steady as its purple-white beam lifted Fossil from the ground. Slowly but steadily, it reeled in the struggling, wailing Super Villain. His holographic form shrank ever smaller as it neared the Blaster – then was swallowed completely. The beam cut out.

As his Multivision Specs wiped off, Matt docked the Cell Blaster's hexagonal face with the *Chronicles*' cover jewel, to inject his captive into it. He detached the Blaster and watched Fossil's image, trapped in a Life Cell, sink slowly into the depths of the jewel.

'A broken heart . . .' said Matt with satisfaction, '. . . and a one way ticket to the Villain Vault!'

As Matt stowed both book and Blaster, Gomez came hurrying up. Roxie, too, was back on her feet.

'We did it!' Matt grinned at them.

Roxie looked mightily relieved. 'Only just!' she said. 'I was in real trouble . . .' She put an arm around Gomez, and gave him a squeeze. 'But my *hero* saved me.'

Gomez looked bashful. 'Oh . . . I . . . it was nothing,' he mumbled awkwardly. Then a huge grin lit his face. 'OK, OK, I admit it – I was *awesome*!'

Matt chuckled. 'Gomez, I'm impressed.'

Suddenly, a purple light fell over the gorge. Matt looked up to see the portal that had brought him to the Sea of Sands snaking down from the sky – a sure sign that, for now at least, his work in the Multiverse was done.

Matt sighed as his Multivision Specs reactivated. 'I'm running late,' he told his two friends. 'Home tuition.' He pulled a face. 'Later, guys!'

As the mouth of the portal swept low enough to lift Matt from the ground, Roxie and Gomez returned his farewell wave. A moment later he had been sucked in and whisked away. The portal quickly withdrew back up into the blue sky, then vanished.

'Hey, did you hear that, Roxie?' Gomez had a smile from ear to ear. 'He's *impressed*.'

Praise from a Hatter Hero was high praise indeed.

22

No Rest for the Wicked

Tenoroc clutched the arms of his stone throne with bony fingers, and tried to focus his fading power on the Life Cells floating before him. He had fanned them out in an arc, in order to browse through them. His narrowed eyes scanned the Super Villains' images hungrily.

'Cyclops . . . yes . . . perhaps *he* . . . would be best . . .' muttered Tenoroc between laboured breaths. 'Or . . . would Minotaur . . . finish . . . the wretched . . . boy . . . more quickly . . . ?'

Doctor Fossil's defeat had hit Tenoroc hard, draining his limited energy. He was on the brink of exhaustion. But pure fury was keeping him going.

He was determined to get rid of Matt Hatter.
It was becoming his one, obsessive goal.

Craw hovered awkwardly nearby. The little
gargoyle was anxiously watching his master's efforts
to rally his strength. He could tell from the way

the floating Life Cells were wobbling and bumping into one another that Tenoroc was barely managing to keep them in the air.

'Erm . . . master,' began Craw hesitantly. He settled on the ground and waddled warily up to Tenoroc. 'Might it not be a good idea for you to . . . er, well . . . *rest* for a little whi–'

'*REST?*'

Tenoroc's shriek made Craw cringe away. 'Well, yes, master,' he croaked, cowering. 'It's just that, well, erm . . . don't you think that otherwise, there's a chance you might, you know, collapse or–'

'I shall not rest, Craw,' raged Tenoroc, 'till I am rid . . . of that infuriating . . . interfering . . . *Hatter*!' He brought a gnarled fist slamming down on the arm of his throne, sending a tremor through the Sky Prison's rocky ground. The jittery Craw hurriedly backed away – and promptly fell on his stony backside.

Tenoroc's fit of temper spent the last drop of his energy. Giving in to exhaustion at last, he slumped back in his throne. His yellow eyes closed and he fell still, barely conscious.

With Tenoroc's levitating powers no longer at work upon them, the collection of Life Cells immediately dropped from the air. They rained down on poor Craw's head. He let out a series of pitiful squeals as they bombarded him. When the last Cell had ricocheted off his stone snout, he got back to his feet and cast a grumpy look at his zonked out master.

'Well, don't say I didn't warn you!' muttered the little gargoyle. Then a cheeky grin spread slowly across his ugly face, as he considered how nice it was, for once, to get the last word.

One Step Closer

Matt waited for the bookcase to revolve part way, then stepped through the revealed opening on to the Coronet's first floor landing.

Time to get back to normality, he thought, with a slight pang of regret.

He was already back in his ordinary clothes. All his Hatter Hero gear – Multivision Specs, action outfit and Cell Blaster – was safely stowed inside the *Chronicles*, which he held in one hand. As the secret doorway to the Screen Two corridor sealed behind him, Matt saw the amber glow in the book's cover jewel fade to the faintest of glimmers.

One area of the landing wall was hung with

pictures. Matt crossed to stand in front of one
of them. It was a portrait of his grandfather.
Matt looked up fondly at the painting of the
silver-haired adventurer.

'I just booked Doctor Fossil, Grandpa,' he said quietly. 'That's another one of Tenoroc's bad guys out of the game. And I won't stop till I've booked them all, and you're back home safely – I promise.'

The sound of squealing startled Matt. Marlon came scurrying across the landing towards him. The little fur-ball sprang on to the bottom ledge of the portrait's frame, and began chittering at Matt frantically.

'Hi there, buddy. What's up?'

Marlon clamped one paw over his mouth.

'What? Stop talking? Why?'

Marlon jabbed his other paw repeatedly in the direction of the staircase.

Matt turned – and was alarmed to see Mrs Crumpepper watching him from the foot of the stairs. He instinctively slipped the *Chronicles* behind his back.

How long has she been there? Did she hear me talking to Grandpa? Or see me use the secret door?

The old lady came towards him. The expression on her face gave nothing away.

'Hello, Mrs Crumpepper,' said Matt sheepishly.

The old lady gave him a hard stare.

'It's about time, young man! I've been looking for you for the last hour!'

An hour! Matt still found it crazy how time passed so differently in different dimensions. It had seemed much longer than that in the Multiverse.

'I was beginning to ask myself where in the world you'd got to,' continued Mrs Crumpepper. Matt thought he saw her gaze flit to the bookcase and back. Her mouth curled in a half-smile. 'But perhaps that was the wrong question . . .'

Before Matt could be sure what she was hinting at, her expression became stern once more. 'There's no time for your lesson now. I have another student waiting. Besides, I seem to have mislaid my worksheets . . .'

Marlon belched, covered his mouth with his paw, and looked awkward.

'. . . so I'll see you tomorrow, Matthew. And I expect you to study hard in the meantime!'

With that she turned on one wheeled heel and glided away.

Once he and Marlon were alone, Matt let out a sigh of relief.

'C'mon, Marlon,' he said wearily. 'I'd better do what she says. When it comes to scary prehistoric creatures, Terrorsaurus Rexus Rex has nothing on The Crumpepper!'

And he set off for his turret room, with his furry pal right by his side.

ACTION FIGURES

FULLY
ARTICULATED
DELUXE
ACTION
FIGURES

 Every Super Villain includes a radio frequency Life Cell that
interacts with Cell Blaster and Chronicles Villain Vault toy

AVAILABLE NOW!

www.matthatter.com